THE PREQUEL TO

THE STORMY ROAD TO CANTERLOT

HASBRO and its logo, MY LITTLE PONY and all related characters are trademarks of Hasbro and are used with permission. © 2017 Hasbro. All Rights Reserved. MY LITTLE PONY: THE MOVIE © 2017 My Little Pony Productions, LLC.

Excerpt from *My Little Pony: Daring Do and the Marked Thief of Marapore* copyright © 2016 HASBRO. All Rights Reserved.

Cover illustration by Katharine Henry-Rodgers.
Cover design by Ching N. Chan.

Little, Brown and Company
Hachette Book Group
1290 Avenue of the Americas, New York, NY 10104
Visit us at lb-kids.com
mylittlepony.com

First Edition: August 2017

Little, Brown and Company is a division of Hachette Book Group, Inc. The Little, Brown name and logo are trademarks of Hachette Book Group, Inc.

The publisher is not responsible for websites (or their content) that are not owned by the publisher.

Library of Congress Control Number 2017943153

ISBNs: 978-0-316-43192-7 (hardcover), 978-0-316-43193-4 (ebook)

Printed in the United States of America

LSC-C

10 9 8 7 6 5 4 3 2 1

THE PREQUEL TO

THE STORMY ROAD TO CANTERLOT

by Sadie Chesterfield

Little, Brown and Company
New York • Boston

PROLOGUE

Tempest Shadow stood on the deck of the airship, looking down at Canterlot. The royal castle stood in the middle of the capital. She was hidden in the clouds high above. Nopony could see her. Nopony even knew she was there.

"It's an impressive city," she said, turning to Grubber. "But we have our chance. The Friendship Festival is happening soon."

"You think that would be a good time to steal the magic from the princesses?" Grubber asked. He sat next to her on the deck of the ship, talking in between bites of his muffin.

"The perfect time. We can descend from the airship to be safe," Tempest said. "There will be so many ponies in Canterlot during the festival, and everypony will be busy and having fun. We'll take them all by surprise."

"Genius plan," Grubber said.

"Now let's take one last look around. We should find out exactly where the entrance to the castle is, and what each of the princesses looks like. The more we know about Canterlot before the Friendship Festival, the better."

"But don't I need a disguise?" Grubber asked.

It felt like years since Tempest Shadow had met Grubber. The short, round creature was less than half her size, with a tuft of white hair and piercing blue eyes. She hadn't seen a creature like him before, in Equestria or anywhere else.

She grabbed two cloaks from the airship cabin and draped one over herself and one over Grubber. Then she ordered the ship down toward Canterlot. They'd dock on the outskirts of the city and make their way to the center. Who knew what they would find there...?

CHAPTER ONE

The young Unicorn walked through the forest, her two best friends right beside her. Glitter Drops and Spring Rain were Unicorns, too, and together the three of them liked to practice their magic. Every morning they'd venture out into the forest or explore the mountains by their small town, taking a break now and then to play ball.

"There it is," the young Unicorn said as they stepped into the clearing. She stared into the sky.

Canterlot was high above them. The capital of Equestria was perched in the mountains and could be seen for miles around. The three friends had never actually been there, but they'd heard hundreds of stories. The city was filled with ivory towers and waterfalls, shimmering spires and majestic views. Most important, it was the home of two of the three princesses, and a common spot for them to meet.

The three princesses were Alicorns, or Unicorns with powerful wings. Princess Celestia and Princess Luna controlled the sun and the moon, and Princess Cadance was the ruler of the Crystal Empire. She had been Princess Celestia's apprentice when she was younger.

"Do you think we'll ever get there?" Spring Rain asked.

"Of course we will," the young Unicorn said. "And who knows…"

Glitter Drops smiled. "Maybe one of us will become a princess one day, too."

"But first, Princess Celestia's School for Gifted Unicorns," the young Unicorn said. "Where all the most talented Unicorns learn to focus their powerful magic. We'll get there someday; I know we will."

The young Unicorn couldn't admit it to even her closest friends, but she thought about Princess Celestia's school every single day. She dreamed about studying in Canterlot, of learning to make magic that glowed and sparked with power. She'd work as hard as she could to make Princess Celestia proud. Sometimes she even imagined becoming an Alicorn herself. Would she ever be given wings? Could she ever be that powerful?

There were entrance exams every spring. The young Unicorn hoped she'd be ready when they came around one moon. She wanted to attend the school as soon as she could. It was hard waiting for something you wanted so much.

"Let's practice," she said, turning to Glitter Drops and Spring Rain. "Let's levitate the ball."

Glitter Drops's horn sparked and glowed. She took the ball from her satchel and sent it flying off into the woods. The young Unicorn darted after it, weaving in and out of the trees. She could just see the ball up ahead, glowing in the air. It was like the bouncy balls other ponies tossed back and forth, only this one was special. If she focused her magic, she could make it float and glow with a beautiful white light. It looked like the moon.

"I can't keep up!" Glitter Drops called out. She was running as fast as she could through the forest, but the ball was always a little ahead of her. She laughed as she ran, clearly loving the way the wind felt in her mane.

Spring Rain darted out in front of the young Unicorn. She raced across the ground to the ball, but she stumbled and fell. She hadn't been concentrating hard enough, but that wasn't her fault. It was tough to concentrate on her magic, run really fast, *and* keep her eyes on the ball.

The young Unicorn galloped out in front of both of her friends. The ball was up ahead.

She was so close. She just had to run a little faster....

"Where'd it go?" Spring Rain's voice called out. "It disappeared!"

The young Unicorn stopped at the mouth of a cave. The ball had floated inside. She could still see the glowing light, but it was dimmer now. The ball was somewhere in there, deep in the mountain.

"Oh no..." Glitter Drops stopped right behind her. She peered inside. The cave was so dark they couldn't see past the opening. "Who's going to go get it?"

Glitter Drops and Spring Rain turned to their brave friend. The purple Unicorn might've been the youngest, but she was always the bravest of the three. She'd talked to the hydra when they went to Froggy Bottom Bogg, and she had found her way through the Everfree Forest on her own. Whenever something scary happened, her friends always looked to her first.

"I'll be right back," the young Unicorn said. Then she ventured into the cave, trying to follow the dim light from the ball.

Inside, she could hardly see anything. The ball was somewhere up ahead, around a sharp corner, but she couldn't make out the floor of the cave. She stumbled over a rock and fell, landing hard. When she finally got up, her shoulder hurt.

"This isn't as easy as I thought it would be...." she said to herself, rubbing the sore spot on her side. She went slower now, being careful with each step. "Just a little farther...."

She was getting closer. As she turned the corner, she saw the ball floating in the air. That whole part of the cave was lit up now. She could see everything perfectly.

It looked like some creature had been living there. There were scraps of food and a warm, cozy bed. She reached up, grabbed the ball, and tucked it behind her front leg. When she turned back around, there was an ursa minor standing right in front of her.

She didn't have time to react. The bear roared in her face. She ducked underneath its foreleg, trying to get away, but it chased after her. She didn't move more than a few feet before it struck her with its giant paw. She went flying across the cave, her head knocking into the wall.

She got up as fast as she could, knowing the bear would be right behind her. As she got closer to the entrance of the cave, she could see Glitter Drops and Spring Rain waiting for her.

They were both staring inside the cave, trying to see what was happening.

"Run!" she yelled. "There's an ursa minor!"

Spring Rain and Glitter Drops turned around and darted off through the forest. The young Unicorn followed them, relieved when she was finally out of the cave. She'd dropped the ball at some point along the way, but it didn't matter. She had to get as far away from the ursa minor as she could.

She didn't stop running until she was out of the forest and saw Spring Rain and Glitter Drops standing in the field up ahead. She turned back, looking into the trees to make sure they were safe. After all that, they were finally alone. The bear hadn't followed them.

"I went all the way to the back of the cave," the young Unicorn said. "I found the ball, but then, when I turned around, the ursa minor was right behind me. It chased me, and then I fell, and then..."

Glitter Drops and Spring Rain just stared at her. Their eyes were wide, and their expressions were serious. They looked like something was horribly wrong. The young Unicorn glanced down at her hooves, making sure she wasn't hurt. She looked over her shoulder at her tail and mane. Everything seemed fine.

"I don't think I'm hurt," she said. "Just a few scratches..."

"I don't know how to tell you this...." Glitter Drops said, her eyes watering. "It's your horn."

The young Unicorn reached up and touched the front of her head. Her horn was just a small, jagged stump—the top half had broken off. Her eyes immediately filled with tears.

"No," she said, shaking her head. "No—it can't be. What's a Unicorn without her horn?"

"I'm so sorry." Glitter Drops hugged her friend.

"It'll be okay," Spring Rain added, wrapping her front leg around the young Unicorn's other side.

The tears streamed down the young Unicorn's cheeks. She'd lost her horn. All her magic was contained within it. How would anything ever be okay again?

CHAPTER TWO

The young Unicorn and her two friends set off through town, Spring Rain walking on one side of her and Glitter Drops walking on the other. She'd waited weeks, then months, for her horn to grow back, but nothing had happened. This was the first time she'd left her house since the day at the cave, but Spring Rain and Glitter Drops had told her it would be okay. She still couldn't help but feel nervous, though. Every time she looked at her broken horn she started crying.

She'd pulled a hat down over her head, and nopony seemed to notice anything was different. She waved at everypony inside the market, and everypony waved back. They passed their friend Moonglow, who was planting tulips outside the art gallery.

"What a lovely hat!" Moonglow said. "The flowers on it are beautiful."

"Thank you, Moonglow," the young Unicorn called as she trotted past.

"See?" Glitter Drops asked. "Is it really that bad?"

The young Unicorn shook her head. "You were right. It feels good to be out and about."

As they got to the clearing, Spring Rain looked around and took a ball out of her satchel.

There weren't many ponies near them. "Want to try it?" she asked. "It couldn't hurt. . . ."

At first the young Unicorn wasn't sure what she was talking about. But then Spring Rain lifted the ball a few inches off the ground, levitating it in front of her.

"Oh, no . . . I shouldn't," the young Unicorn said. "I haven't used my horn for magic since the accident. I don't even know if it'll work."

"You're the bravest Unicorn we know," Glitter Drops said. "I always tell stories about my friend who isn't afraid of anypony or anything. You can do whatever you put your mind to."

The young Unicorn glanced back toward town. There wasn't anypony around. Maybe it wouldn't be the worst thing to just try. She hadn't had the courage to since her horn broke.

"Ready?" Spring Rain said, dropping the ball back to the ground.

The young Unicorn nodded and took off her hat. Glitter Drops and Spring Rain both trotted out in front of her, farther into the clearing. She focused her magic on her horn, trying to lift the ball off the ground. Her horn sparked. She stood there, waiting for it to work as a few more sparks shot out toward the trees.

Her power was building—she could feel it—and suddenly her broken horn shot off an incredible show of light. It was burning hot, and turned everything it touched to ash and dust. A whole row of trees burned underneath it.

"Watch out!" Glitter Drops cried as the young Unicorn stepped forward, trying to control it. She stumbled, and as her head turned, she scorched a patch of grass.

When her horn finally stopped shooting sparks, she stood there, trying to catch her breath. Spring Rain was lying in the grass. She'd bumped her head. Glitter Drops was hiding behind a tree. The young Unicorn reached out her hoof to help Spring Rain stand, but her friend flinched. When she stared up at her, her eyes were full of fear.

"I didn't mean it," the young Unicorn tried to explain. "I don't know what happened...."

Spring Rain stood on her own. She brushed herself off and offered her friend a small smile. "It's okay. It was an accident."

Glitter Drops came up next to them, but the young Unicorn noticed both her friends didn't get too close. They kept glancing at her horn. They seemed afraid of her now. "Are you okay?" Glitter Drops asked Spring Rain. "That was a serious fall."

"I think I'm all right....It was just scary," Spring Rain said.

"I'm so sorry," the young Unicorn said. "It's something about my horn....It doesn't work right anymore."

"It's okay," Spring Rain said again, but she seemed sad. "Let's just go back home."

Glitter Drops and Spring Rain turned back toward town, and all the young Unicorn could do was follow. She knew Spring Rain was just frightened, but she couldn't help feeling like everything was her fault. Her horn was broken, her magic was gone, and things would never be the same between them. Everything had gone so wrong after that day at the cave.

She walked beside her friends, her hat snug on her head again. Glitter Drops and Spring

Rain didn't say anything else. The young Unicorn's mind was racing: Would she ever get her magic back? How would her friends be able to trust her? And how could she stay in her town when everything felt so wrong?

CHAPTER THREE

The moons passed. The young Unicorn spent more and more time at home, reading and baking and doing anything that didn't remind her of the magic she'd once had. Glitter Drops and Spring Rain still came by to see her every once in a while, but they never asked her to go to the clearing with them to practice magic. They never even mentioned her horn. Instead they pretended as if that day in the cave had never happened.

So when they knocked on her door one morning, she hoped maybe something had changed. Maybe they weren't afraid of her after all.

She flung open the door.

"Where to?" she asked. She'd already put on her hat. It had been so long since she'd seen her friends; she couldn't help but miss them and all the fun times they'd had. She'd just go with them to get some apple cider, and then she'd come home. She wouldn't even talk about magic or what they used to do in the clearing.

"Actually..." Glitter Drops began slowly. She looked a little sad. "We wanted to talk to you about something."

"What do you mean?" the young Unicorn asked.

"We took the entrance exams for Princess Celestia's School for Gifted Unicorns," Spring Rain said. "We wanted to tell you before you heard it from any other pony."

The young Unicorn tried to hide the hurt in her expression, but she could already feel her eyes welling up with tears. Since the day she'd broken her horn, she'd tried to bury her dreams down deep in her heart. She hoped that one day her horn would grow back, along with her magic, and she could go to Princess Celestia's school, but until then she tried her best to forget. Sometimes she wouldn't even glance up at Canterlot. It was hard to see the city glittering in the sky and not think of all the possibilities of a future there.

"I didn't realize they'd happened already," the young Unicorn said. "I just…I hadn't thought about it since…"

"We know," Glitter Drops said. "And we know your horn is going to grow back soon. It's only a matter of time. But we felt like we had to take the exams this moon. The term starts in the fall."

"So you're going?" she asked as she tried to steady her voice.

"Yeah," Spring Rain said. "But you'll come next moon. We'll all be together again soon. And we'll come back to visit all the time. We'll still be friends."

"Right," the young Unicorn said. "Of course. We'll always be friends. I'm happy for you."

The young Unicorn put on her best smile, even though she was hurting. Glitter Drops and Spring Rain looked relieved that she was being so nice about it. She said good-bye to her friends, and they promised that they'd see one another the next day. She told them they were going to have the best time at Princess Celestia's school. Then she closed the door and started to cry.

The young Unicorn put on the cloak she had pieced together and stared at the bag on the floor. She pulled it onto her back, knowing she had no other choice. If she stayed, she'd always be different. The Unicorn with the broken horn. The Unicorn without magic. The Unicorn whose friends left her behind. What kind of life would that be?

She stepped outside, pulled up her hood, and turned back one last time to say good-bye to her cottage. She'd leave tonight, for good. There were other places she could go, and other ponies who might accept her. She couldn't keep pretending she was happy here. This town no longer felt like home.

As she started off into the night, she reminded herself of the worst part. She'd been the brave one that day in the forest. She'd volunteered to go into the cave to get the ball so her friends didn't have to. She'd yelled to Glitter Drops and Spring Rain, telling them there was an ursa minor inside so they wouldn't get hurt. She'd done everything right.

And what did she have to show for it? What did she get for being a good friend?

Nothing, she thought as the lights from the town grew smaller in the distance. *There's nothing left for me there.*

CHAPTER FOUR

After days of traveling, the young Unicorn's bag was nearly empty. She had only a few apples and carrots left, plus a small jug of water. It was hard traveling alone. She could only carry so much by herself, and she ran out of supplies faster than if she were traveling in a group.

She'd wandered through the White Tail Woods, spending nights under trees that gave her cover while she slept. After that, she'd made a wrong turn, crossing the train tracks into the San Palomino Desert. She'd been there for four days and had drunk almost all her water. Now she stood on the outskirts of Appleloosa. She'd have to venture into town if she wanted more food.

She pulled the hood down over her broken horn and held on to the edge so it wouldn't blow off. The town was flat and windy, with tumbleweeds rolling across the streets. A few ponies waved as she walked past. She waved back, enjoying how normal it felt to be there. She was just another pony, strolling through the town. There was an apple orchard just beyond the buildings. Rows and rows of apple trees, all in bloom. It reminded her a little of home.

The young Unicorn ducked inside the general

store, looking for supplies. She grabbed three bundles of carrots, a big bag of apples, and another jug of water. It would last her a week, at least. She dropped them all on the counter in front of the clerk.

"You're not from around here, are you?" the pony asked. She was purple, the same color as the young Unicorn, and had a beautiful blue mane. "First time in Appleloosa?"

"Yup, first time. I've been on the road for a while," she said, paying for the supplies with some bits. "I needed to stop somewhere to get more food."

"Well, I hope you'll stop for a lot more than that," the clerk said. "Appleloosa has so much to offer. Every week we have shows on the town stage, and there are plenty of Wild West dances. Everypony's welcome."

"Wild West dances?" the young Unicorn asked.

"Oh, they sound more complicated than they are. It took me only a few minutes to learn, but much longer to get good. I think there's one tonight. . . . Would you like to be my guest?"

She stared at the pony, not sure why she was being so nice to her. She'd gotten used to ponies staring at her broken horn a little too long, or inviting her to things because they felt bad for her. But this pony seemed like she genuinely wanted to be friends.

The young Unicorn shook her head, remembering where friendship had gotten her before. "I better head out soon," she said. "Thank you, though."

"Well, at least promise me you'll stop by the Salt Block before you leave," the pony said.

"It's my favorite place in town. They've got the best apple cider on this side of the Rambling Rock Ridge."

"I promise," the young Unicorn said, remembering the cider at home. She'd have to stop in just to see for herself. She put the supplies in her bag, fastened it shut, and said good-bye to the nice clerk. Then she strode out into the street to find the Salt Block.

It was impossible to miss. It seemed like the busiest place in town. A crowd of ponies stood under the green-and-beige-striped awning, while others pushed through the swinging doors. She could hear ponies laughing and talking from outside.

She went in, and immediately, she felt better. She'd forgotten how much she missed being around other ponies. Everypony seemed to be having a great time. She grabbed a stool and ordered an apple cider.

"What do you think?" a pony with a blue western hat standing next to her asked. He watched as the young Unicorn took a sip. "They say it's the best apple cider on this side of the Rambling Rock Ridge, but I'm not totally convinced."

"It's pretty good."

"Ah." He paused, looking at her bag. "Where are you headed?"

She stared into her mug. She couldn't tell him the truth: that she'd only know where she was going once she got there. So she looked at the map on the wall and picked somewhere random.

"I was just going to visit friends near Galloping Gorge," she said.

"That's a long way from here," replied the

pony. "But you're in luck. Me and my band of ponies are headed to Vanhoover. You could travel north with us if you like."

The pony pointed to a group sitting at the table behind him. They were eating apple chips covered in caramel sauce. They looked like a friendly bunch. One of the girl ponies was telling jokes, and the whole group laughed loudly.

"I could go with you?" the Unicorn asked, not sure if she'd heard that right. She'd been alone on the road for so many days, and for so much longer before that, when she was back home. The idea of traveling with others did sound appealing. She wouldn't have to worry about supplies nearly as much. . . .

"Why, sure!" the pony said. "I'm Tumbleweed, by the way. Come on over and I'll introduce you to my friends."

"I'm...Caramel Chip," the young Unicorn said, not wanting to tell the stranger her real name. She followed him over to the table and smiled when she saw the group.

"Hi, all," Tumbleweed said. "The young Unicorn here is going to join us on our way to Vanhoover. She's heading up to...where did you say you're going?"

She glanced at the map, trying to remember the place. "Galloping Gorge! I'm heading up there to see friends."

"*Ahhhh,*" a pony with a purple mane said. "Well, we've got plenty of supplies, and we could always use extra company. The more the merrier."

The young Unicorn was about to sit down when the swinging doors of the saloon blew open. A gust of wind ripped through the room, blowing her hood right off her head. She stood there, in the center of the saloon, her broken horn exposed for everypony to see.

"Say, what happened to your horn?" one of the ponies asked.

She pulled her hood up to cover it. Her whole face turned from purple to red. She'd come so many miles from home, but she was still the same pony, still the Unicorn with the broken horn. She darted out of the Salt Block before anypony could say anything else. She ran through the street, her head down, not stopping until Appleloosa was far behind her.

CHAPTER FIVE

The young Unicorn walked for days across the desert. She kept going, putting one hoof in front of the other, through dozens of sunrises and sunsets. She tried not to think about what had happened at the Salt Block in Appleloosa. She tried to stop picturing the other ponies' faces when they saw her broken horn.

She couldn't figure out how many days had

passed. How many weeks had it been since she'd traveled through the outskirts of Equestria? She was out of food, and she only had a few drops of water left in her jug. There was a small city in the middle of the desert, just a cluster of buildings against miles and miles of sand. She'd have to stop there. If she didn't get water soon, she'd be in trouble.

Most of the buildings were boarded up, and there was only one small restaurant with dirty windows the young Unicorn could hardly see through. The streets were lined with different creatures who appeared to have come down on hard luck. They were sleeping in alleyways and doorways. Many of them had tattered shawls covering their head and shoulders. The young Unicorn couldn't even see their faces.

She crept to the window of the restaurant

and peered inside. Through the dirt and grime she could just barely make out a few figures sitting around tables. Some were drinking cider; others were eating plates of gross-looking food. She tugged extra tightly on her hood as she stepped inside.

As soon as she sat down, she realized she had much more to worry about than her horn. The place stunk of sour cider and rotting food. Everyone in there seemed sad. Their clothes were ripped and torn. Many of them were sitting alone.

Behind her, two rough-looking creatures ate the last of their food. One was looking at a newspaper. "Ugh...more news from Equestria. Can't stand it."

"Makes me mad," the other said. "They're up there, sparkly streets and fancy clothes.

Princesses and princes. It's like the rest of us don't exist."

The young Unicorn swallowed hard. "Uh, yeah…" she muttered under her breath. She hated to admit it, but she understood what the creatures meant. Since she left her town, every day had been a struggle to survive. She'd tried so hard to forget about Canterlot…and Celestia's school…and the three princesses. It was too painful to think that other ponies had easier lives. That they lived in castles with views of all Equestria.

The waiter came over, and the young Unicorn ordered something off the menu, which was stained with bits of food. She struggled to eat the meal, even though it tasted horrible. After she was done, the waiter let her fill up her jug of water. When he finally put the bill down on the table, she went into her bag, looking for her bits.

"No ... this can't be ..." she said, pushing her hoof through a hole in the bottom of the sack. She must've ripped it at some point on her journey. All her bits had fallen out of the bottom. "I'm sorry—I've lost my bits. I don't know how I'll pay."

A customer at the table next to her laughed. "Likely story! We've heard that one before."

It seemed like the whole restaurant was laughing now. The waiter, an older creature with just a few teeth, shook his head. "You'll have to work off your meal, then." He pointed to a pile of dirty dishes in the sink. "Plenty for you to do around here."

The young Unicorn glanced around the

dingy restaurant. She hadn't wanted to stay even an hour in this city, and now she'd have to stay days. Her stomach twisted at the thought. She stood and went to the sink, starting her first shift at the tiny place.

+ + ✦ ◗◖ + +

The young Unicorn ended up working in the restaurant for moons. She lived on the streets of the small city, which was called Drungar. She ate food she'd take home from the restaurant and slept in an abandoned shack she'd discovered in an alley. It had taken her only a week to work off the bits she owed for her meal, but she never seemed to make enough to leave the city. It felt as if it took forever to build up enough savings to buy supplies and continue her journey.

She'd finally taken off into the desert, hoping she'd find somewhere else besides Drungar. Anywhere would be better than that place. The dank, dirty streets. The smell of rotting garbage everywhere. The piles and piles of dirty dishes that she could never get totally clean. The only good thing about it was that no one seemed to notice her horn was broken. Or maybe they simply didn't care.

The sand stretched out in every direction. Up above, the stars were shining brightly in the sky. It seemed like the best night she'd had in a very long time. As she walked, she noticed a glowing light appeared up ahead. She climbed over a hill and saw a burning wreck in the valley below. It looked as if some sort of ship that had caught on fire and crashed there in the desert. She started toward it, looking down at some of the charred pieces. There were burnt supplies and giant chunks of the ship deck. She walked deeper into the wreckage, noticing something sparkling in the blackened sand.

There was a large gem sitting in the rubble. She picked it up and turned it over in her hooves. It looked like it was worth more bits than she'd ever be able to make at that restaurant. Even better, when she held it, she could feel that it possessed some sort of special power. But for what? How could she use it?

Before she could think about it more, there was a rushing sound overhead. She turned to see a huge airship floating above her. A long plank was lowered, and a small, round creature started down it. He was short with a tuft of white hair. He had piercing blue eyes and wore black armor with a strange symbol on the front—almost like a face. When he set foot on the sand, he pointed in the Unicorn's direction.

"There it is! The Misfortune Malachite! That gem belongs to the Storm King!" he yelled.

The young Unicorn tucked the gem into her bag, not wanting him to take it away. Maybe she hadn't figured out what it was for, but she'd found it. It was only fair that she get to keep it.

"Does it?" she said. "He should have taken better care of it, then."

"Hand it over, lady!" the creature said. "Or face the Storm King's wrath! That gem's got a lot of magic, and he needs it!"

So she was right. The gem did possess a special power. Maybe she could use it to grow back her horn. She turned and started off again, but the creature called after her.

"Halt! Stop right there!" he yelled, but the

Unicorn continued on. "Not another inch! Seriously, I'm telling you to stop walking. Do not go any farther. You must give that back."

She only walked faster, trying to get away. The creature didn't look like he would hurt her (or that he could hurt anyone, really), and she'd never seen him before. Who was he to tell her what she "must" do?

But before she could go any farther, she heard the sound of footsteps. Many, many footsteps. She turned, realizing the creature wasn't alone. There was a small army behind him. These creatures were taller and much scarier looking. Some had horns; others had long claws. They all had white hair and scraggly faces with sharp teeth.

The Unicorn had no time to think. She took

off across the desert, running as fast as she could. It wasn't long before one of the creatures caught up to her. She spun around to face him. The creature looked surprised that she was ready for a fight. He was twice her size, with a hunchback and two sharp fangs. He sprang forward and tried to grab her bag from her back, but she darted out of the way at the last second. He tumbled headfirst into the sand.

Before she could take off, another creature came at her from the other side. She bucked back, landing a kick in the creature's stomach. He folded over in pain.

There were more creatures pouring out of the airship. She turned and ran as fast as she could. The creatures were much bigger and slower, and it wasn't long before she had a good lead. She turned back one last time to see the small, round creature watching her. She stared at him, daring him to follow, then took off into the night.

+ + ⸮⸮ + +

Leaving the desert wasn't easy. She'd been able to outrun the scary creatures with the white fur, but then they'd followed her in the airship. She had to hide beneath a rock and wait as they circled above. It took an hour before they finally left.

As soon as she was sure they were gone, she made her way out of the desert. She couldn't travel through the open stretches of sand anymore. Now that the small army knew she had their gem, they would be searching for her. And the desert would be the first place they'd look.

Instead she continued on until she came to a small village. A sign outside the main gate read KLUGETOWN. Tiny cottages and shops lined the narrow streets. She walked, keeping her head down, and ducked into a store to buy some supplies.

She set her haul down on the counter and listened to the two creatures working there. They were busy and hadn't noticed her when she walked into the store. "There are rumors that the Storm King's expanding his empire," a large purple creature said. "He wants more power."

"How much power does he need?" the other creature asked. He was shorter, with long green hair. "I feel like I already see those airships everywhere."

They both turned, suddenly noticing the

Unicorn waiting. The purple creature was silent as she put a few bits on the counter. They didn't start talking again until after she left the store.

Once she was outside, she ducked down an alleyway and pulled the gem from her bag. They'd spoken about the Storm King and his airships.... This gem was his. But what kind of magic did it hold? And how could she use it on her own?

As she held it between her hooves, she tried to focus. It had been so long since she'd used her broken horn. It glowed and shot sparks across the alley. Then she stared at the gem, hoping she could activate it. Suddenly, she heard someone say something.

She turned, thinking someone was behind

her, but no one was there. It took her a second to realize the voice was coming from the gem itself. She leaned closer, listening to the quiet whispers. *"Beware the Misfortune Malachite,"* the voice said. *"As soon as I held it, terrible things began to happen."*

The Unicorn shook her head, shocked at what she was hearing. A gem that gave you bad luck? She didn't believe in such a ridiculous thing. But a different voice whispered another warning.

"Rid yourself of this stone at once! You must!" the voice said. *"Or your life will change for the worse!"*

The Unicorn tucked the gem back into her bag. She wondered if maybe this Storm King was playing a trick on her. Maybe he wanted her to think the gem was bad so she wouldn't keep it. Besides, she'd already lost her horn and left the only town she'd ever known. How could things get worse?

She glanced out the alleyway, noticing a caravan passing by. There were a dozen covered wagons leaving the city with supplies. She hopped onto the back of the last one and hid behind some crates so no one would see her. Then she closed her eyes and slept.

CHAPTER SIX

The next morning, the young Unicorn peered out over the Forgotten Hills. She'd slept for hours in the covered wagon but jumped off it as soon as she heard an approaching attack. She felt a little bad, but quickly got over it. She knew it was everypony for themselves in this world. She made it out safely and continued on her own. Unfortunately, she had left her cloak in the process, so she shivered as she climbed high into the mountains, knowing it would be another whole day of searching for a place to call home. For the first time in a long time, her loneliness felt unbearable.

She checked her bag to make sure the gem was still there. Then she stood, staring down at the town and scenery below. She had to get as far away from the desert, and Klugetown, as possible. She'd travel west and seek shelter there. Lately, she couldn't seem to remember just how long it'd been since she left Equestria for good.

The mountain was steep. As she made her way down it, toward the Bleak Valley, her steps were unsure. Her hooves kept slipping on the gravel, and she often had to stop and steady herself.

"Easy there, Hobble Hooves," a voice said. "You don't want to slip and fall."

The young Unicorn spun around, looking for the speaker. She froze in place. A small, round creature was perched on a rock above. He had spiky white hair and bright-blue eyes. He was the same creature who had stepped down off the airship, the one who'd sent his scary army after her. She glanced around, looking for an escape, but there was nowhere to go.

"Are you . . . the Storm King?" she asked.

The creature laughed. "I'm not," he said. "But I know him well. I'm his . . . *assistant*."

He was eating a thick slice of cake, the crumbs falling down the front of his armor. He would take a bite, chew, and stare at her. Then he did the same thing all over again.

"Where'd you come from?" the young Unicorn asked, peering around. She'd been in this part of the mountain all morning, and she hadn't noticed a single sign of him. She'd even checked for tracks, to be safe.

"I was just out for my morning stroll," the creature said. "Fresh air is good for the mind, you know. Really clears your head. And there you were. What's a pony like you doing all the way up in the Forgotten Hills? You must be very far from home."

"I'm not a pony; I'm a Unicorn," she said without thinking.

The rotund little creature hopped down from his rock and stood in front of her, staring up at her broken horn. "*Ahhh*, yes," he said. "I see. Had a little accident, did you? It doesn't seem like it has slowed you down much. I saw how you fought off our army."

"You shouldn't have come at me like that. I was just defending myself."

"I'm not mad," he said. "I was impressed. You can keep the Malachite, just for that brave little stunt. You won it fair."

Maybe it was because he wasn't a pony, or maybe it was because it was so odd, being stuck in the middle of the mountains with a complete stranger, especially one from whom she'd stolen a gemstone, but the Unicorn suddenly felt like she could talk to him.

"An ursa minor," she said. "That was the accident. He broke it."

The little creature winced.

"My magic is gone. I've tried to focus, but without my horn..."

"It can't be that bad," the creature said.

"It really is."

"I don't believe it. You seem braver than a Hippogriff army. Let's see."

He stood there, waiting for her to show him. The young Unicorn hadn't tried using her horn since the day in the clearing with her friends.

"It's not safe," she said. "I shouldn't."

"I'm not scared." The creature plopped down on another rock, as if to say, *Go on. I can wait here all day.*

The Unicorn took a deep breath. She closed her eyes to focus on her horn. It glowed. Within seconds it shot out a long stream of sparks and fire, scorching the side of the mountain. She stumbled around, trying to control it, but it was too powerful. It took a few minutes before she was able to stand up again.

She wiped the ash off her nose and cheeks. She was so embarrassed she could barely look at him. Did he believe her now? Did he understand how dangerous her power was? Maybe she had fought his army, but that didn't mean much now, did it?

"That was..." the creature started. "Amazing!"

The Unicorn just sat there, stunned. "Really? We could've gotten really hurt...or worse."

The creature just waved his paw, as if that didn't matter. "Small details," he said. "There's a lot of power in what you can do. It really is incredible. That combined with the bravery I saw the other night...You're a very special Unicorn. Do you know that?"

She blushed. "Thank you..."

"I know the Storm King would be amazed by your skill. You should come meet him."

The young Unicorn's stomach twisted in a knot. Something didn't feel right. Just the other night this creature had sent his army after her, but now he was inviting her to meet his friend. It all seemed a little odd.

"No?" he asked, noticing the Unicorn's silence. "Then I should get back...."

The creature stepped away and started over the hills. The Unicorn had only just begun talking to him, and now he was leaving. She didn't even know his name. Maybe she wasn't sure if she should go wherever he was going, but that didn't mean they couldn't talk some more.

"Wait—you didn't introduce yourself," she said. "And can you tell me more about this Storm King?"

The creature spun around.

"Oh yes, that was pretty rude of me. I'm

Grubber, and the Storm King is my master—though I prefer *boss*, really. It has a nicer ring to it. He's one of the most powerful creatures I've ever encountered. Grows even more powerful by the day."

Grubber began to walk off again. The Unicorn stared at the hill below, dreading the thought of going down it alone. When was the last time someone had told her she was special? That she wasn't dangerous, but amazing? That she could be more than a dishwasher in a dingy restaurant?

Besides, she had nowhere to go and nopony to see. What did she have to lose?

"Wait for me," she called out. She slipped along the path as she hurried to catch Grubber.

He turned around and smiled. Just then, an imposing figure appeared.

CHAPTER SEVEN

The Unicorn knew who it was. "Oh," she
said.

"You know," a booming voice said, "you've
been leading me on quite the chase!"

Grubber seemed much quieter now. The
young Unicorn looked around, quickly scan-
ning for him, but he was nowhere to be seen.
She took a deep breath and looked the Storm
King in the face.

He was three times the size of the Unicorn, with thick white fur and piercing blue eyes that were similar to Grubber's. His chin stuck out from his face, as did two sharp bottom teeth. In fact, his face looked a lot like the symbol on Grubber's jacket.

"So, what are you, little creature? Are you worth my time?"

"I am a Unicorn," she began nervously. "I've come a long way in search of powerful magic." She continued, "I've faced many dangers to find it."

"I'll say! You've done a pretty good job, too!" the beast said, staring down at the Unicorn. She stood up straight under his gaze. She wanted him to think she was as special as Grubber had said she was.

"Let's see it," the Storm King ordered.

The Unicorn, feeling more nervous than she had since they'd arrived, glanced at the approaching storm clouds. She focused on her horn, letting it spark and glow. Then the flames shot out in all directions, the air filling with bright-white light.

"Not bad," the Storm King said. He scratched the back of his head with one long finger. "Reminds me of this party I went to once in Zorgarth. Fireworks and strobe lights. I was dancing to the music, feeling it truly when—"

"What?" the Unicorn asked. The Storm King realized that maybe this wasn't the best time to talk about his crazy times in distant lands.

"I mean . . . very good," the Storm King said.

The young Unicorn stared down at her hooves. The snow around them had melted from her sparks. One patch of land was completely black.

"I'm so sorry...." she said, looking at the Storm King. "I didn't mean to do that. I just—"

But the Storm King started clapping. "Don't be sorry," he said. "That was amazing. You are special."

"I am?" the young Unicorn said.

"You are welcome in my castle anytime. Grubber will prepare a room for you in the east wing." The Storm King paced back and forth. Then he turned, as if he were looking at the Unicorn for the first time. "Your horn...it's broken."

Her hoof went up to cover it. She wished she had her cloak. She'd left the caravan so fast she'd left it there.

"I had an accident...." the Unicorn said.

"I could fix that for you, you know." The

Storm King said it as if it would be as simple as making a cup of tea.

"You could fix my horn?"

The Unicorn couldn't help but smile. For so many months she'd watched her horn in the mirror, hoping for any sign that it would grow back. She'd focused, trying to grow it herself, but nothing worked. This might've been the chance she needed. Maybe she was meant to be here. Maybe she was meant to find Grubber. The Storm King would fix her horn, and she'd return home, take the entrance exam, and be in Canterlot by the following fall.

"Of course I can help," the Storm King said. "But you'll have to do something for me first. A little quid pro quo..."

"What's that?" the Unicorn asked. She'd never heard those words in her life.

"Well, I could use your help with something, and you could use my help with something. It would be an exchange. I think this could work out nicely, that's all...." The Storm King held up his staff. The rod was twisted, and there was a pretty blue stone wedged in the top. He had the same symbol on his armor as Grubber had on his jacket.

"The Misfortune Malachite?" she asked. She pulled it from her bag and held it up.

The Storm King smiled. "You know that gem has terrible bad luck. You should never have taken it in the first place."

"I don't believe in bad luck," she said. "But I do believe in magic. And I need this gem to restore mine." She self-consciously touched her broken horn.

"Is that all?" the Storm King asked. "Well,

I can do that for you. Once I've finished conquering, I'll have more power than any other creature in the world!"

The Unicorn tried to contain her excitement. "Is that why you're searching for magic? For power?"

"What other goal is there?" the Storm King asked, baffled. "Power! Control! These are the only things worth seeking in this world. I'll fix your horn and restore your magic." He slowly extended his large claw. "*If* you pay my price...."

The Unicorn passed the gem to the Storm King.

The Storm King crushed the gem in his hand, turning it to dust. "Well, I believe in bad luck, by the way. And I don't need any if I'm going to conquer more lands. But I think you can help me with something more specific...."

"What?" the Unicorn asked.

"High atop Mount Aris lives the Queen of the Hippogriffs. Do you know the Hippogriffs?" he asked.

She nodded. Of course she knew the Hippogriffs. A Hippogriff had the head, wings, and feet of an eagle, but its back legs and tail were that of a pony. They were some of the most beautiful and powerful creatures in the sky.

"She's in possession of a magic pearl." He smirked as he said it. "It has transformation qualities that could really give me power and finally make this staff work. No bad luck at all. And the queen and I...we've had our differences, so I don't see her just handing it over to me any time soon. That is where you come in."

"You want me to go up there and ask her for it?" the Unicorn said.

"I want you to get it any way you can," he said. "Grubber will help you."

Then he continued on. "Go to Mount Aris, find the pearl, and bring it back to me. Then I'll make your horn whole again."

The Unicorn thought about it. She knew it would be wrong to take the queen's pearl, but things had been so hard since she'd left her small town. She never stopped thinking about what her life would've been like if she had her horn and magic back. She'd be able to return home and reunite with her friends Spring Rain and Glitter Drops. She'd study with Princess Celestia. She'd have her life and her dreams again.

The Hippogriffs were brave and fierce, but hadn't she been known as the bravest Unicorn there was? Getting the pearl wouldn't be hard when she'd already fought an ursa minor. She had to go to Mount Aris. She had to at least try.

"I'll do it," she said. "When do you need it?" the Unicorn asked.

"Yesterday," the Storm King replied. "But I realize you may need time to prepare. Grubber!" the Storm King called out. The creature appeared from behind an outcrop, this time his arms full. "Get our friend some armor and introduce her to the Storm Creatures. You'll bring them with you when you go to Mount Aris."

"We'll leave tomorrow night," Grubber said. He handed something to the Unicorn. It was the same black armor the Storm King and Grubber wore. It had the bright-blue symbol on the side—two lines, like the Storm King's face. "Come on; I'll take you to the castle. I'll let you sleep on the top bunk."

The winds were getting stronger. The Unicorn turned to leave, but the Storm King called out to her.

"One last thing," he said. "What's your name? I don't think I ever caught it."

"Tempest," the Unicorn said. She liked how it sounded out loud and immediately decided she'd keep this name. "Call me Tempest Shadow."

The Storm King smiled down at the sad Unicorn with the broken horn. Yes, she'd be his tempest. She'd storm Mount Aris and bring him back the pearl. Or else...

CHAPTER EIGHT

These are the Storm Creatures," Grubber said, walking Tempest Shadow into a great hall the next day. "You all have...um, *met* before. They'll be joining us on our mission."

The creatures stood there, facing her. Now that she was looking at them up close, she realized they all looked like strange versions of the Storm King. They had the same white fur around their faces, and they wore the same black armor with the blue symbol. But the beasts had sharp, pointy faces and beady blue eyes. One was huge, with paws like a lion's. Two long tusks curled out from his nose. (She thought he was the one she had kicked, but she couldn't be sure.) Another stood on his hind legs. He was shorter than the rest, with thick arms that looked as if they could smash someone with one blow. They all peered down at her. None of them spoke.

"Do they need to come?" Tempest asked. Then she turned to the creatures and shrugged. "No offense...."

One of the Storm Creatures crossed his arms over his chest. He was definitely offended.

"The Hippogriffs are very powerful. We should bring them just in case. They're good to have on your side in a fight." Grubber leaned in and whispered in Tempest's ear, "Now, this is where you give them a pep talk."

"Right," Tempest said, not really sure what to say. She and Grubber had come up with a plan, but she wasn't exactly expecting to lead the group. And definitely not the small army she had just fought days before...

"So...Storm Creatures," she said. "We leave for Mount Aris tonight. You'll wait on the airship while Grubber and I enter the castle. The Queen of the Hippogriffs has a magic pearl that we need to get for the Storm King. Grubber and I will find it, and then we'll count on you to be there when we make our escape. But remember: We want this to be as quiet as possible."

The Storm Creatures looked confused.

"*Quiet* isn't really their thing," Grubber whispered.

"Grubber and I will take care of everything," Tempest said. "You'll wait on the ship. We'll just need you as backup."

They stood there, staring at her with their beady blue eyes. They didn't seem excited about staying on the airship, but they didn't seem mad about it, either. Grubber inched toward her. "This is where you lead them to the ship," he whispered.

"Okay," Tempest said, letting out a deep breath. "Let's ready the ship for our journey. Storm Creatures, head out!"

The creatures all turned at the same time and marched out of the great hall. They climbed down the hill and marched across the long bridge away from the Storm King's castle. That was when Tempest saw the ship for the first time.

It was bigger than the one she'd seen in the

desert, and it was nestled in a swirling storm cloud. Set against the sunset, this airship was one of the most impressive things she'd ever seen. She remembered then what Spring Rain and Glitter Drops had always said to her— how she was the bravest of them all. Tonight, she'd be stronger and fiercer than ever before. She'd lead Grubber and the Storm Creatures to Mount Aris and bring back the pearl. Not for the Storm King, but for herself.

A Unicorn was nothing without her horn.

"Come on," Tempest said as she started up a long, steep staircase to the city of Hippogriffia. Grubber was behind her, but the hike was too much for him. He was breathing heavily, and he kept stopping on every other stair to rest.

They'd left the ship far below. The Storm Creatures weren't happy to not be going up to the city, but Tempest promised she would call for them if they were needed. Almost as soon as she said it, she hoped that wouldn't happen. She just wanted to get in, get the pearl, and leave. The faster this was over, the better it would be.

She kept walking up the stairs, turning back once to make sure the ship was hidden. Mount Aris was perched high up in the clouds. They'd parked the ship far below, then covered it with a giant storm cloud. From where she was standing, it just looked as if there was rain at the base of the mountain.

"No one mentioned the stairs," Grubber said, huffing behind her.

"We're nearly at the top," Tempest said. "Just a little farther."

When they finally arrived, they looked past the beautiful gates. Inside, the city was all stone, with carved pillars and statues of Hippogriffs. An official-looking Hippogriff sat on the other side of the gate, guarding it.

"Who goes there?" he called as soon as she spotted Grubber and Tempest.

Tempest had a shawl around her shoulders. She and Grubber had disguised themselves with rags and old pieces of clothing they'd found in the castle kitchen. The long, tattered shawl covered Tempest's armor. Grubber wore a black hooded cloak that was ripped at the seams.

"I'm sorry to bother you...." Tempest let the shawl fall from her head, exposing her broken horn. "We've gotten lost. We've been traveling for days, and I'm afraid we're very weak."

"How does that concern us? Do you know where you are?" the Hippogriff asked.

Grubber shook his head, pretending he did not. He was sitting on the steps, and every other second he coughed. He really did look like a sick and weary traveler.

"This is the city of Hippogriffia," the Hippogriff said. "Only Hippogriffs are allowed inside these gates."

"We wouldn't ask for help if we didn't really need it." Tempest stared into the Hippogriff's eyes. She knew she was lying, but she was used to that by now. It was a survival skill. There was no way they'd be let in if they didn't have a convincing story. She'd tell the truth after tonight. After they got the pearl. After the Storm King fixed her horn.

Without another word, the Hippogriff lifted

off into the air. He was a magnificent blue creature with impressive wings. He went up into the stars, then swooped down and disappeared behind one of the buildings.

"Do you think it worked?" Grubber asked, peering through the gate. There were stone statues lining the street. They were all Hippogriffs posed in different positions.

"I don't know…." Tempest said. She stared up at the buildings. It was late, but she could see light in a few of the windows. Why couldn't they let them in for just one night? Was the city really so strict they'd leave them outside?

She turned and sat down on the steps. Tempest glanced back at the city. The Hippogriff was nowhere in sight. "How long should we wait?" she asked.

"As long as we have to," Grubber said. "We can't go back without the pearl."

There was something about the way he said it. It seemed as if they weren't allowed to fail. Would the Storm King let them back into the castle if they didn't have the pearl? Or would Tempest be banned forever?

She heard the sound of the Hippogriff's wings against the sky. The giant creature swooped down and landed on the other side of the gate. Then he unlocked it and let the doors swing open.

"The queen has granted your stay in the city," he said. "But only for the night. What are your names?"

"I'm Cherry Pie," Tempest lied. She couldn't use her new name. Not when they were going to steal the pearl. "And this is . . . Mort."

"I'm Stratus Skyranger," the Hippogriff said. "Come—follow me, and we'll get you food and a warm bed."

He walked down the stone street. Tempest gazed up at all the statues, high buildings, and carved pillars. Grubber plodded along behind her. She turned back just once, and his eyes were wide.

Their plan had worked.

CHAPTER NINE

The soup was delicious. Tempest didn't realize how hungry she was until she was sitting at the table in the castle's great hall. She finished her whole bowl in just minutes.

"So I see you enjoyed your meal." Stratus strode in from the main hall. "Now I'd like to take you to meet the Queen of the Hippogriffs. You are her guests for tonight. I think it's only proper."

"Yes, right," Tempest said, standing up. Grubber followed behind her as they made their way down a long hallway. She pulled the shawl tighter around her shoulders, making sure her armor was hidden.

Stratus stopped at two huge doors at the end of the hall. Two guards were standing on either side of it. They stepped back once they recognized Stratus, approaching with Tempest and Grubber.

"Your Majesty..." Stratus Skyranger lowered to one knee and bowed his head.

A large Hippogriff was lying on a long velvet lounge chair. Her eyes were covered with a green mask, and her head was wrapped in a soft velvet scarf. She pulled the mask off her eyes when she heard Stratus's voice.

"Interrupting my beauty ritual again?" asked the queen. "Stratus Skyranger, how many times do I have to tell you? A queen has to look her best for her subjects. I mean—"

She stopped, noticing Tempest and Grubber standing there.

"My queen," Stratus Skyranger said, stepping aside so Tempest and Grubber could come forward, "this is Cherry Pie and Mort. They're the travelers I told you about. I thought they should meet the queen who has generously opened her doors to them."

Tempest and Grubber both got down on one knee each, following Stratus Skyranger's lead.

"Thank you for all your help," Tempest said.

"We don't often let strangers past the city gates." The queen stood as she said it. She was much taller than Tempest thought she'd be. Her giant wings hung by her sides. "But Stratus here told me how desperate you were. It seems you've had a long, difficult journey."

"We have," Grubber chimed in. "Very long and very difficult. Very long. Yup."

"Where did you travel from?" The queen stared down at Grubber, waiting for him to answer. His blue eyes went wide. Tempest could tell he was panicking.

"From the Forgotten Hills," Tempest lied, standing up. "We'd been living there for a long time but decided to leave to find a better home. But then we got lost...."

The queen studied her as she spoke. This didn't bother Tempest. She'd become used to lying. As she told the story it felt true—at least some parts of it. She had been in the Forgotten Hills with Grubber. And she had left to find a better home.

After a pause, the queen smiled warmly.

"You'll have to stay tomorrow morning," she said. "My daughter would love to meet you. She's always telling me we should let other creatures into the city. She loves hearing different stories about what it's like outside the city walls, and if I'm being honest, I think she could use some friends her own age. How many times can she ask Stratus to play dolls with her before he gets bored?"

"We'd love to meet her," Grubber replied. He offered a sly smile.

"Stratus will get you whatever you need," the queen said. "We want our guests to be as comfortable as possible."

Tempest was about to say something else, but then she noticed a shell on the table next to the queen's chair. The shell was open, revealing a sparkling pearl inside. She glanced sideways at Grubber. He'd seen it, too.

"Right, thank you," Tempest said, trying to seem normal. She knelt again to say good-bye. "We appreciate all you've done for us, Your Majesty."

Grubber offered a small bow, and they both followed Stratus out.

"You'll be staying in the north wing," he said.

As soon as Stratus's back was turned, Grubber stared at Tempest. His eyes were wide. "Did you see that?" He whispered it softly so only she could hear him.

Tempest nodded. The pearl was right there,

right next to the queen's bed. It had been only a few feet away.

Tonight, while the queen was sleeping, it would become theirs.

CHAPTER TEN

The room was dark. Tempest could barely see Grubber, even though he was right next to her. He was snoring loudly, his lips fluttering with every breath.

"Grubber," she said. But he didn't wake up. She nudged him with her hoof. "Grubber!"

He sat up in bed, scared. "What?!"

"It's time."

Tempest turned to her bed. She took the two

fluffy pillows they'd given her and stuffed them under the blanket. Then she stood. It looked like she was still sleeping, her face hidden by the covers. If Stratus checked on them, he would think they were still there.

Grubber took one pillow and stuck it under his blanket, making it as round as he could. "Spitting image," he said, staring at the lump. Then he pulled on his tattered cloak. "Let's go."

He started out the door, turning in the direction of the queen's room.

"Wait," Tempest said. "It's better if I go alone. Besides, it's going to take you a while to get to the city gates with your legs."

"My legs?" Grubber asked, offended. He stared down at them.

"They're tiny," she said. "That's all. Why don't you get a head start and meet me there?"

The truth was that it would be so much easier if Grubber wasn't with her. She could sneak in, get the pearl, and sneak out. She was worried Grubber might try to steal the queen's jewelry, or accidentally wake her. She could just picture him knocking into some huge vase and all the guards running to see what had happened. It wasn't worth it.

But Grubber looked upset. "Really? I thought it was you and me. A team."

"It is," Tempest said. "But that's why I need you by the gate...to keep a lookout. As soon as I get the pearl, I'll meet you there; then we'll go down the stairs together."

Grubber nodded, and then he shuffled down the hallway. He stayed close to the wall so he wouldn't be seen.

Tempest went in the opposite direction. She

peered around the corner, looking at the doors to the queen's room. A guard stood on either side. It was risky, but her powers were all she had right now. She closed her eyes and focused on her horn. It sparked and glowed and she could feel that something was working.

Down the hall, she noticed a mirror hanging over a table. She focused as hard as she could, then shot the sparks. They hit the mirror, knocking it onto the floor, where it smashed into a hundred pieces. The Hippogriff guards ran toward it.

"What was that?" one asked. Tempest hid behind some curtains, staying out of sight. The guards went in different directions to search for the culprit. As soon as they were gone, Tempest ran toward the queen's bedroom and slipped inside. Moonlight streamed through the window, lighting up parts of the room. The queen tossed and turned in her sleep. Her eyes were covered by a blue velvet mask.

Tempest spotted the pearl on the table beside the queen's bed. She crept over to it as quietly as she could. Cold air blew in from outside, sending a chill down her spine. She pulled her shawl around her to keep warm. Then she was there, right in front of it, the pearl shining in its shell. She reached out and closed it. Then she tucked it into the front of her armor.

"What are you doing with my pearl?" a voice asked.

Tempest turned around and stared right at the queen. She was awake and sitting in bed. Her mask was off, and she flew into the air, her wings spread wide. She looked terrifying.

"Do you dare come into my home and try to

steal from me?" her voice boomed through the room. "Nocreature wrongs the Hippogriffs. You will pay dearly!"

Tempest was so startled she couldn't respond. She let the shawl drop from her shoulders and ran as fast as she could for the door. As she barreled down the hall, she heard the queen yelling behind her.

"Stop her! She has the pearl!"

CHAPTER ELEVEN

Within seconds, an alarm sounded. It blared through the halls and echoed out into the streets. Suddenly, all Hippogriffia was awake.

Tempest darted through the castle, turning just in time to see two guards charging at her from the west wing. She ran through the great hall and into the city square. The guards were right behind her, getting closer by the second.

She ran past a castle, past the marble pillars and beautiful statues of Hippogriffs, and toward the city gates. Grubber was standing beside them, waiting for her. As she sprinted toward him, he looked up, staring at something behind her. His eyes were wide.

"Tempest! Watch out!" he yelled.

She glanced over her shoulder. The two giant Hippogriffs were almost upon her. They swooped down, their claws outstretched. She fell to the ground, covering her head with her hooves. She was sure this was it. There was no way out. She'd be captured and taken prisoner for what she'd done.

Oomph! There was a dull thud of something crashing into the Hippogriffs, then shrieks as they flew through the air. When Tempest finally peeked through her hooves, she couldn't believe what she saw. Dozens of Storm Creatures were in the streets of Hippogriffia. Hearing the alarm, they'd pulled the ship up to the city to defend her. Some were still scaling the walls. Others worked together to bust through the main gates.

Stratus was battling two Storm Creatures at the same time. He'd fly up into the air, then swoop down to take on one. The other kept jumping on her back, trying to pin down her wings.

Tempest glanced at the castle, watching as the Hippogriffs flew out one by one. The queen was in the front of the flock, her wings spread against the sky. Her face hardened when she saw Tempest in the city square.

"There she is!" the queen yelled, leading the group. "Look at her armor. She was sent here by the Storm King to steal the pearl! Don't let her get away!"

Tempest scrambled to her hooves. Minute by minute, more Storm Creatures broke into the city, knocking over pillars and statues. One leaped onto the back of a flying Hippogriff. Two others broke into one of the buildings and came out with armfuls of treasure.

Grubber was lost among the chaos. He was desperately trying to get back to the ship, but he was so small it was a risk to take even one step. He tried to get around a fight between a Storm Creature and a green Hippogriff, but then the Storm Creature tossed the Hippogriff across the square. One of her wings hit Grubber. He flew into the side of a building and landed with a thud.

A huge purple Hippogriff swooped down on

him, its claws reaching out to pluck him into the sky. It was just inches away from snatching him up and bringing him back to the castle. Tempest had no choice. She ran forward, knocking the Hippogriff out of the way. But now she was in the middle of the fight. Two more Hippogriffs came at them from either side.

"We're trapped," Grubber said.

They were backed against a wall. A pillar had fallen over, boxing them in. The queen was getting closer. The Storm Creatures were so busy battling the other Hippogriffs they didn't notice Grubber and Tempest in the corner of the square, trapped and helpless.

The queen descended upon them. Her eyes were filled with fury.

"Give me the pearl!" she demanded. "Or I will take it myself."

Tempest could feel the pearl was still there, tucked in the front of her armor. She glanced into the square, hoping one of the Storm Creatures would save her, but they were all fighting their own battles. It was up to her to save herself.

"Come and get it, then," she said, springing to her hooves. She got into a fighting stance. "The pearl is mine now."

"Not likely."

The queen swooped down on Tempest. Tempest darted to the side, avoiding her. Then they were both on the ground, face-to-face. The queen stalked forward. She swept her wing out, pinning Tempest to the wall with all her weight. Tempest could barely breathe.

The queen reached into Tempest's collar and

pulled out the pearl. She held it right under Tempest's nose, her eyes filled with fury. "You have come here and taken advantage of our kindness. You have stolen from us. You have brought the Storm King's army here and destroyed our city."

The queen lifted off the ground, preparing to take flight. Her front claws were outstretched. She dove, about to bring Tempest and Grubber with her, when two Storm Creatures moved in. One battled with her, dodging blows, while the other climbed onto her back and tried to pin her down. The queen struggled, then broke free.

"My loyal subjects—retreat!" The queen called out. "Retreat!"

She looped around toward the castle, her

daughter right beside her. A dozen other Hippogriffs followed. Some were injured from the fight. Others came down from the roofs of buildings or perches high above. One emerged from a pile of rubble near the broken gate.

The Hippogriffs flew as fast as they could toward the castle. Tempest followed, watching as her hopes of getting the pearl went with them. The queen and the others rushed into the building, and the queen uttered something Tempest couldn't hear. Then the whole building filled with bright light.

By the time Tempest got to the entrance, the Hippogriffs were gone. The castle was completely empty. The Hippogriffs had vanished without a trace.

Tempest saw the destruction they'd caused. The castle arches, which had fallen to the ground. The broken statues and pillars. The gaping holes in the walls where a Storm Creature had burst through.

They had done this. They had destroyed Hippogriffia.

CHAPTER TWELVE

You go first," Grubber said, nudging Tempest with his finger. They stood in the doorway to the throne room. The Storm King was facing the window, as he always did. One hand was curled around the arm of his throne and the other held his staff, the blue stone glittering in the light.

Tempest knew she should be the one to tell him what had happened. But for some reason she couldn't move from that spot. The whole journey back to his castle she kept rehearsing how she'd explain it, and how she'd respond to his disappointment, but now that she was actually there she could barely move.

While she was working up the courage, the Storm Creatures marched in from the ship. They lined up against the walls and waited for the Storm King to give them orders. His throne slowly spun around.

"I see that you've returned," he said, eyeing his army as he stood. "And you've been very busy." The Storm Creatures' fur was ripped out in places. A few of them had lost pieces of armor in the battle, and one had a chipped horn. They all looked tired. They were standing with their shoulders hunched forward, their eyes on the floor.

"We have, Storm King, we have," Grubber said.

The Storm King's gaze moved to Tempest, a hint of a smile on his lips.

"*Ahhhh*, Tempest Shadow," he said. "Come, let's see it. Show me the pearl."

Grubber nudged Tempest again. She stepped forward and took a deep breath.

"I tried my best," she said. "We tricked the Hippogriffs into letting us into the city. They had us stay in the castle, and I was there—I was in the queen's room. I was holding the pearl...."

"I don't like where this is going," the Storm King replied.

"It all happened so fast," Tempest went on. "There was an alarm, and then the Storm Creatures came. The queen, she took the pearl back."

"Where is it now?" the Storm King said, pacing back and forth. He let the end of his staff drag against the floor.

"I don't know," Tempest said. "They all just disappeared. I tried to get it back, but I didn't want to hurt anyone. I feel guilty that—"

"Guilty?" the Storm King asked. "That's your problem, Tempest. You still believe, deep down, that the world can be fair. You want to get the pearl from the queen, but you don't want anyone to get hurt. You want to get your horn back, but you don't want to do anything you don't want to do."

"I just . . ." Tempest trailed off.

"You are not a child anymore," the Storm King said, taking a step toward her. "Every creature for themself. That is the true law of the land. Learn it and live by it, and then maybe one day you will succeed."

The Storm King turned to the assembled Storm Creatures.

"Go now," he said. "Clean yourselves up. And next time, when you're supposed to do something, do not disappoint me."

The creatures marched out of the throne room. Tempest listened to their steps echo against the stone, until only she and Grubber were left. She took a step forward, her eyes filling with tears. The Storm King was already looking out the window again, as if they weren't there.

"Storm King…" She said it so softly she could barely hear her own voice. "Will you still fix my horn?"

"You want me to fix your horn?" the Storm King asked, as if it were a silly question. "Is the pearl here? Is it in my staff right now, with its awesome transformational powers? Has it made me stronger than before? Am I turning into a bugbear? Or a cipactli? Or a jackalope?"

The Storm King spun around, showing Tempest that he was not.

"No ..." Tempest said slowly.

"Then that is your answer," the Storm King snapped. "You do something for me; I do something for you. You do nothing for me; I do nothing for you. And actually, if we're keeping tabs here, you owe me one night's rent."

Clutching his staff, the Storm King started to walk out. Tempest's heart leaped into her throat. She had to do something—she had to say something to change his mind. She couldn't stand the thought of her horn being broken forever. She didn't want to leave here and return home. She wouldn't.

Every creature for themself, she repeated in her head. It was true—hadn't she learned so that day in the cave? Hadn't she remembered it all those weeks and months after, when her magic grew out of control? When was she going to put herself first, and do what was best for her alone?

"You wanted the pearl so you could transform," Tempest started. "But what if there was something even better than that? What if you could control the most powerful magic of all?" Tempest asked. She could see the Storm King's expression changing. He liked her idea; she knew he did. He wasn't smiling—not exactly. But he was close to it.

"Well, well, why do you ask?"

"Equestria," Tempest said. "It is full of magic. Crystals! Princesses!"

"The princesses of Equestria," the Storm King repeated.

It was too late for her now. They'd destroyed Hippogriffia, and the queen knew who she was. Wherever she went from now on, she'd always be running from what she had done. The Storm King was right; it was better to just worry about yourself. If she had her horn back *and* the power of all three princesses, she'd be the most powerful Unicorn in all Equestria. She wouldn't need any school or any friends or any masters to help her. Not anymore.

"I can see it," the Storm King replied. "The Storm King controlling the magic of an entire land in his staff. Yes, you must return to

Equestria and bring me the magic of the three princesses."

"And then you will fix my horn?" Tempest asked.

"And then I will fix your horn."

Tempest turned to leave, sharing a small smile with Grubber.

"But this time," the Storm King called after her, "do not fail me, *Commander* Tempest."

CHAPTER THIRTEEN

Tempest trained with Grubber for weeks. She knew if she was going to go up against the Alicorns in Canterlot she'd need to perfect her own dangerous magic. She'd need to make sure that she could count on herself.

"So, let's see it one more time," Grubber said. "Just for good luck."

He stood at the edge of the Great Hall. He'd borrowed some of the Storm Creatures' armor, so she could just see a tiny set of eyes peering out from behind a giant chest plate. They'd had a few accidents early on, and Grubber refused to take any more chances. He was still trying to grow fur back on a spot on his bottom.

Tempest grunted. Her horn sparked, shooting off fiery white light. She didn't close her eyes anymore when it happened. Instead she watched as it sparked and flamed in front of her. By focusing so intensely, she'd learned to make them even stronger than before.

"Good!" Grubber said, peering out from the armor. "Looks great."

Tempest eyed a banner hanging from the ceiling. The banner had the Storm King's logo on it, the two jagged blue horns. She pointed her head in its direction and fired. There was an explosion of light and flames, and the cloth banner turned to ash. It was so heavy it fell to the ground, covering everything with a thin layer of dust.

When she was done, she bowed her head. Grubber stepped out from behind his armor and clapped, the whole hall filling with the sound.

"You…are…on…fire!" he said. "Literally. Good work, Tempest. You've come a long way."

"I have," Tempest said, but for the first time in her life, she didn't need any other creature to tell her that. She knew how powerful she was. And soon, all Equestria would know it, too.

"Come on, Grubber," she said, starting toward the airship. "We leave tonight. I need to find out as much as I can about Canterlot if we're going to take the castle."

She smiled, feeling stronger than ever before.

It was only a matter of time before they descended on Canterlot. When she faced off against the princesses, she'd be ready.

Tempest stepped off the airship, turning to say good-bye to Grubber. "Make sure you stay hidden," she said. "And if I'm not back in an hour, come find me."

"You won't even know I'm here," he said.

Clouds spilled out around the airship, swirling up and over its front. In just a few seconds the ship completely disappeared. They'd parked it on the outskirts of Canterlot, and now Tempest was making her way through the capital's narrow streets. She turned back one last time to be certain Grubber was hidden.

Tempest couldn't remember just how many

moons it had been since she left Equestria. She was certain *some* things had changed, but a lot seemed the same. The streets of Canterlot were quite crowded. Ponies sat outside cafés, sipping tea and chatting. One stood in the window of a shop. She dusted the marble statues with a huge purple feather duster. Tempest stopped to watch, and a glamorous Unicorn brushed past her, her pale-pink mane fluttering in the breeze.

Tempest pulled her dark cloak closer, making sure it was covering her horn. Canterlot was exactly how she'd always dreamed it would be. There were tall, glittering spires that seemed to touch the sky. Theaters and art galleries and coffee shops with elegant ponies sipping elegant drinks. It was unlike any place she'd ever seen before—shinier and prettier, and full of all the fanciest ponies. The worst part was that she didn't belong there. Not with her shabby cloak and broken horn. Not even close.

She kept a low profile as she walked through the city, her eyes fixed on the castle. She stopped at a coffee shop to listen to a few ponies talk. They were going on and on about a wedding that was happening soon. Tempest knew it wouldn't be an event big enough to attract all the princesses. Another group of ponies chatted about a new boutique that had opened up. Another pony was telling her friend about her plans for her birthday. Tempest sighed, frustrated with how useless the information was.

Up ahead, she noticed a group of ponies sitting by a fountain and enjoying the sun. She was going to just walk past, but then one of them said something about an Alicorn named Twilight Sparkle. It sounded like she had been crowned a princess of Equestria not too long ago. Tempest paused in a nearby doorway to listen to their conversation.

"Her magic really is unparalleled," a pony with a sky-blue mane said. "It's no wonder she was one of Celestia's favorite students. I can't wait to see what she does next week."

A pony with a shimmery gold mane smiled. "Music and dancing and desserts. It'll be the biggest event in the history of Canterlot."

"Princess Twilight is in charge of planning everything," a lavender pony said.

"Are Celestia and Luna moving the sun or moon for the festival?" somepony asked.

"I don't think so," the blue pony said. "I think they'll just be there."

"Along with every other pony," the one with the shimmery gold mane said. "Did you know hundreds of ponies are invited to the Friendship Festival? I don't know a single one who's not going."

Just then a group walked down the street. The crowd parted around them. In front was a purple Alicorn. She had a dark-purple mane with a pink streak in it. Behind her were a pink pony with a balloon cutie mark and a blue pony with a rainbow mane. Everypony broke out into excited whispers.

"There they are!" somepony cried out. "Princess Twilight, Pinkie Pie, and Rainbow Dash."

Twilight Sparkle and her friends passed out fliers to the group Tempest had been eavesdropping on. They strolled past, handing her a flier, too. *You are cordially invited to the Friendship Festival!* it read in cheerful script.

"We're so excited to see you all next week,"

she said. "This is going to be the best festival in the history of Canterlot!"

Everypony watched as they made their way past. Tempest heard somepony say something about how special they were.

She stared at the flier for the Friendship Festival, feeling angrier than ever. Twilight Sparkle was living the life Tempest had always dreamed of. Living in Canterlot, as a princess, with friends and parties and festivals that were planned just for fun. But what did it matter, anyway? Who cared about friendship when your friends so easily turned away from you? When they left you behind for no good reason?

Tempest tucked the flier in her cloak. The Friendship Festival. It was the perfect opportunity to steal the princesses' magic. All the princesses would have to be there, especially if it was the biggest event in Canterlot's history. And now Tempest Shadow was invited, too....

She turned down a narrow street, winding her way back to the edge of the city. Grubber was waiting for her, and she had to tell him what she'd found out. The Friendship Festival was just one week away. There was so much planning to do. When would they come for the princesses' magic? What was the best way to steal it? They'd have to return to map out the city and make a plan....

When she was almost at the airship, she turned left instead of right and saw a familiar sight. The huge purple-and-white building had giant stairs leading to its entrance. She'd imagined running up them a hundred times before. She'd imagined what it would feel like to walk through the halls with her friends or study in one of those beautiful classrooms, Celestia standing at the board in front of her.

She stared up at the School for Gifted Unicorns one last time before she turned to leave. All she could picture was Glitter Drops's and Spring Rain's surprised faces as she descended on Canterlot in her giant airship. She imagined what they would think when they saw her army, all the Storm Creatures, and watched her take the princesses' magic.

Yes, she thought, a smile curling on her lips. *It will be glorious. . . .*

Ready for more pony-rific adventures?

Turn the page for an excerpt from
DARING DO AND THE MARKED THIEF OF MARAPORE!

Available Now!

CHAPTER 1

On the High Seas

As Daring Do riffled through her saddle-bag, she began to feel queasy. And it wasn't from the rocking of the great ship upon the choppy, churning sea. It was from the realization that all that was left of her rations—which had once been a carefully selected bounty of dried apples, salted carrots, and seed-crusted loaf—was one stale piece of bread. It wasn't enough to feed a filly.

If only her supplies hadn't been depleted during the storm over the Fillyppine Sea, Daring could have held out longer here on board the SS *Blue Peter*. But a life on the water was an unpredictable one, and the currents had thrown the ship far off course. As a result, the adventurer hadn't been able to sneak off board at any port, let alone into a general store to replenish her provisions. The entire crew was starting to run low on necessary supplies.

Of course, borrowing from the ship's galley again was always an option. But that endeavor would be risky. The sailors took careful inventory of their commodities, and if something went missing, Daring Do would soon be discovered. Three days prior, she'd given into temptation and pilfered a potpie from a tall stack about to be served to the crew for supper. Nopony had noticed. Daring had bitten into the flaky, buttery crust and gooey center with satisfaction.

But later that evening, when she was full-bellied and poring over her tattered map of Deep Unknown—a rare guide to the Submerged Temples of Tehuti—Daring Do overheard the cook, Greasy Spoon, chiding his helper, Square Meal, for eating more than his fair share. Greasy had threatened Square that if he didn't fess up, he'd go without meals for the entirety of the next week. Square Meal lied out of sheer desperation and said he'd eaten two pies, chalking it up to Greasy's amazing cooking skills. That seemed to satisfy his boss.

Daring had felt dreadful for the poor colt during the whole episode, but there was no chance she was going to reveal herself now. Daring had heard many a tall tale in seaside cafés of the consequences for stowing away on Captain Pony the Elder's ship, but they were not something she wished to confirm or deny. Although the captain was no pirate, the military stallion had a reputation for treating stowaways worse than Hoofbeard.

Suddenly, the ship lurched. Dirty pots piled in the washbasin clanked against one another, and Greasy Spoon hollered a curse. Daring's already weakened body slammed against the splintered wooden door, squashing her right wing. She groaned in agony. That wing had never been the same since her nasty crash landing in the jungle near the Yucatán Ponynsula. It vexed her more than anything to have an injury.

"Grrrr." Daring gritted her teeth as she inspected the aching appendage. It hurt like mad. Maybe she didn't want to admit it to herself, but Daring Do was becoming fatigued by her many weeks at sea in search of the Crystal Sphere of Khumn. Legend said that the magical item could be found in one of the Submerged Temples of Tehuti, located one hundred fathoms below the surface, held by a statue between two golden hooves, beneath a shining metal rod. It was believed that the Sphere had the power to heal anypony who touched it, no matter the ailment. Too bad the fabled ancient city was even harder to find than the Gallopinghost Islands! Like with most treasures, Daring Do felt an intense hunger to find it and make it hers. Or at the very least, stop it from falling into the wrong hooves or claws.

Though she'd been unsuccessful in her quest thus far, she wasn't giving up forever. Daring just needed to do more research, delving deeper into the murky mysteries of Tehuti and Khumn. Then she'd immediately set out on the open seas again. Next time, with more provisions—maybe even dried peppered pears, a few apple tarts, and a small pillow.

A strong gust of cold air blew into the cabin closet where she was crammed. The rickety old mahogany had splintered off in areas, leaving several gaping holes. It was perfect for spying on Captain Pony and his seafaring ruffians (known as the Royal Navy) on board the *Blue Peter*. Not quite ideal for warmth on the high seas, though.

Daring massaged her tender wing. The high winds on board had been rough— too strong for flying. Even so, Daring would never have risked being seen. Not for just a little stretch. She'd surely have been dumped at the nearest port, which was hundreds of miles away from home.

By keeping out of sight, Daring had made it all the way to her destination in one piece.

She thought of her warm bed back in her little cottage in the woods. Daring racked her brain, but she couldn't remember the last time she'd slept there. Before she'd taken off to find the Crystal Sphere of Khumn, she'd been busy searching for the Talisman of Tenochtitlan. And before that, she was waylaid in the jungle with the injured wing, hunting for Ahuizotl's temple. Things never seemed to slow down for Daring Do, but that was the way she preferred it. As far as she was concerned, an idle life was a boring life. There were always treasures to discover and ponies in distress to rescue!

The boatswain, a strong yellow stallion known as Steel Anchor, passed by the tiny porthole in the door of Daring's hideout. She could tell it was Steel by the way his hooves clunked heavily against the ship's wooden deck planks. In fact, Daring could recognize most of the crew now just from weeks of eavesdropping and paying close attention to their little quirks.

"Hey!" Steel Anchor stopped just outside the closet porthole. "Did you hear about old Mo? He *turned*…"

"That so? Darn shame…" added Sea Storm, a junior deck cadet. The pony lowered his voice to a murmur. Daring pressed her ear against the glass so she didn't miss a word. She wasn't sure who Mo was and what he had turned to, but information was precious—no matter what it was. It sounded like the faint glimmer of something intriguing. Sea Storm continued on, "Always had it in 'im, though. Poor chap had been through a lot with his flank situation and all. Nasty thing. Too bad he couldn't—"

But the conversation was abruptly halted by the call of "Land ho!" It was soon followed by another series of shouts from the rest of the crew, bustling around getting the ship ready to dock. They had finally reached port.

"About time," Daring grumbled to herself. She tossed her map, piece of stale bread, and a stolen flagon of cider into her bag and prepared to disembark. If Daring's calculations were correct, the *Blue*

Peter was currently docked at Horseshoe Bay, a sparkling little sapphire inlet on the east coast of Greater Equestria. Once she had successfully escaped the boat, the journey would take about a day to get home—as the Pegasus flies. The thought of stretching her wings made her feathers itch with anticipation.

It was always strange to walk on land after so much time at sea. But at least she had other options. It was going to be wonderful to be on solid ground again, even if it meant that every step she took was going to make Daring's hooves feel like lead. *Ouch!* she mouthed silently as she tried in vain to stretch her wings. The massage hadn't really helped. Apparently, even flying was going to be a struggle.

Here goes nothing, she thought, and hoped for the best. She tore out of the galley, leaped off the ship, and flew as fast as she could into the chilly azure sky. All but one of the crew was too busy to notice her.

Square Meal, the cook's scrawny assistant, stood dumbfounded, scratching his mane, as the stowaway Pegasus became a tiny speck in the distance. Had he really just seen a gold pony with a gray-and-black mane fly out of the kitchen closet? Square Meal then remembered the missing pie and frowned.

"Playtime's over, Captain Pony!" Daring laughed as the ship became increasingly tiny beneath her, its little sails rolling up like the whole craft was about to be stashed in a filly's wooden toy box next to the blocks and dolls. "Thanks for the free ride!" Daring called out with a tip of her pith helmet, though the seafarer didn't hear it. She was already well out of earshot, swooping through gusts and breezes, feeling as free as a dragon during its first migration season.

Even though she was starving, exhausted, and sore, the golden pony couldn't help but smile as she veered her course homeward. She let the fresh, salty air fill her lungs and thought about what would happen next. Whatever it was, Daring Do couldn't wait to figure it out. There was no time for anything else when adventure was calling your name.

CHAPTER 2

A Cloaked Stranger

When Daring Do finally arrived in the woods the next day, she saw somepony pacing back and forth in front of her humble abode. The tiny two-story cottage had a yellow thatched roof and a little brown polka-dot chimney. It wasn't much, but it was home. For the few days a year she wasn't out searching for lost treasures and stolen amulets, at least. The main reason Daring Do liked the place was because it was unassuming—nopony would ever guess that a world-renowned treasure hunter lived there. Nopony, apparently, except *this* stallion.

The golden Pegasus scurried behind a nearby rock, narrowly avoiding the visitor's attention. She'd had enough experience to know that a random pony was not always a good sign. It could be sinister, some sort of trap. Naturally, Daring wasn't afraid of traps, but observing a situation first gave her the upper hoof. "Watch and learn," she always used to tell A. B. Ravenhoof. "Ponies give away more information about themselves just by existing than you could ever pry out of them."

The cloaked pony knocked on the door again, this time a little louder. He was getting impatient. The stallion pushed his green velvet hood back to reveal an unruly golden mane, deep-set eyes, and broad features. His yellow coat was so grimy, he looked like he'd crawled through a gopher tunnel to get there. Clumps of mud and leaves clung to his mane. He smelled strongly of sweet peppered pears, which was incongruous with his dirty, rumpled appearance. He frowned and trotted over to one of the front windows.

Daring Do craned to see his cutie mark. If she could catch a glimpse, maybe she could identify him as either friend or foe. Luckily, his green cloak kept bunching up and sliding into the arch of his back. When the velvet finally cleared away from his flank, Daring saw that the mark was shaped like a yellow rectangle, with black marks along one side. It was a ruler, the kind used in a classroom. Considering Daring Do's photographic memory for cutie marks, she knew instantly that she had never laid eyes on this pony before. Which made him a wild card, a potential loose cannon. Not to be trusted—only to be observed.

Maybe he was one of Dr. Caballeron's lackeys. The jilted Caballeron had never quite gotten over Daring's refusal to work with him as a team, searching for ancient relics and keeping all realms of Equestria safe from the evil designs of the gargantuan blue dog monster Ahuizotl. Now

Caballeron took every chance he got to throw obstacles in Daring's path. If there was something Daring Do was searching for, it was guaranteed that Caballeron would be two trots behind her, picking up the clues left in her wake and trying to make sense of it all so he could take the prize for himself. He needed her, but the feeling was not mutual. Daring Do worked alone—except under extremely rare circumstances. The Rings of Scorchero were proof that much was true.

But who was this mysterious, bedraggled stranger standing in front of her secret woodland cottage? His odd clothing and distinct, foreign features implied that he had traveled quite a distance to find her.

Daring Do recalled meeting a group of ponies with similar-style cloaks on a journey to the Tenochtitlan Basin in the southern latitudes. Daring Do had been en route for weeks, on her way to ransack the camp of the Ketztwctl Empress, hoping to stop her dark magic from ever controlling the Amulet of Atonement again. However, the landmark Daring had chosen happened to be a wandering tree, and she had unwittingly been traveling farther from her destination every day! Luckily, three young mares from a village called Lusitano, down near the Appleloosan Trail, had found her. They'd noticed the distinctive tree dancing in the distance and guessed it had found a target on whom to play its cruel joke. Daring Do was embarrassed at her ignorance of the species of tree, but she thanked them for their kindness. The ponies had also been generous enough to guide her to the empress, even though it put them at great personal risk. Nopony wanted to go near the empress, for she was known to bewitch random passersby and use them for her dark and twisted plots.

With his similar look, this blond pony could have been one of the noble residents of the same region, but he was still untrustworthy until proven otherwise. Daring Do sensed something was off. Especially with the smell of those peppered pears.

"Daring Do!" he bellowed into the clearing. His voice fell flat against the dense thicket of trees. "If you are anywhere in the vicinity—and I *hope* you are—it would do you well to visit the village Marapore. Before it's too late!" He turned and looked right at her hiding rock, his eyes boring into it as if it were transparent. Daring Do sucked in her breath. His voice was heavy with regret. "It may well be too late already."

"Something to help you study," the pony said, bending down to the porch. He sighed, lingering for a few more moments, his eyes searching the trees. "I wish I could explain more, but we're going to need that brilliant mind of yours if you're going to save us from him. *Please*, come save us, Daring Do." Then he galloped off into the forest with his golden mane flowing and cloak streaming out behind him.

Study hard? Save them? What in the Unicorn Mountain Range was he talking about? Daring emerged from her hiding place and trotted to her front door, her brain working overtime trying to make sense of the newfound puzzle.

"Ooof!" Daring cried out as something on the stoop caught her hoof. The pony could hardly believe her eyes when she saw it. She had just stumbled over an item she'd been trying to find for *years*. It was more precious to her than any gem-studded relics or magical healing crystal spheres. It was a book!

You know how
Tempest Shadow
became the Unicorn
she is....Now read
what happens next!

MY LITTLE PONY

EQUESTRIA GIRLS™

MAGICAL MOVIE NIGHT

NOW ON DVD!